TITLE: BLUE BOOK: THE GREAT UFO PROJECT

AUTHOR: Colonel William Weir

COMPILED BY: Victor Trafford

NOTES: Contains accounts of UFO sightings

BLUE BOOK: THE GREAT UFO PROJECT 

Author: Colonel William Weir
Sourced & Compiled by Victor Trafford

Published and distributed by

ACASHIC INTELLECTUAL CAPITAL PTY LIMITED
PO Box 8030, Subiaco East
WA 6008, Australia
+618 9324 4455
mail@acashic.com acashic@gmail.com

Font size — 12pt, Cambria Paper — Book Cream
Editor in Chief: Michael Garcia

Creative Director & Cover Design: Evonne Hew

Production: Acashic Actuality

ISBN 978-1-105-73472-4

DISCLAIMER

Acashic Intellectual Capital Pty Limited ("the Publisher") asserts the following in regards to the book ("the Work") and the cover ("the Cover"):

The views expressed on any aspect of the Cover and in the Work are solely those of the Author ("the Author"), other writers and or individuals providing them, and do not reflect the opinions of the Publisher, its parent, affiliate or subsidiary companies. Caution is advised when reading or using the Work. The Publisher is not responsible for any damages sustained by the Reader ("the Reader") or User ("the User") of the Work, when reading or using the Work. The Publisher shall not be responsible for any aspect that may result in claims of defamation and invasion of privacy. In all instances the Publisher has relied on the expertise of the Author and has not investigated the matters provided by the Author. The Publisher has no duty to investigate the factual or other basis of the material provided by the Author.

Protection is deemed to include all of the Publisher's products which includes but is not limited to books, web sites, CD-ROMs, DVDs and other media ("the Products") that give advice or provide instructional information – all of which are protected in their own right under appropriate, legally drafted Disclaimers.

Copying or disseminating any information published by the Publisher, electronic or otherwise is strictly prohibited. The Reader should be aware that the text of the Work is subject to change at any time. Uploading of the Work and its Cover without permission of the Publisher is unauthorized and may lead to a conviction as a result of a piracy suit.

The work is provided by the Publisher on an "as is" basis. The Publisher makes no representations or warranties of any kind, express or implied, as to the operation of the Work, its website(s), the information, content, materials or products, included in the Work. To the full extent permissible by applicable law, the Publisher disclaims all warranties, express or implied, including but not limited to, implied warranties of merchantability and fitness for a particular purpose. The Publisher will not be liable for any damages of any kind arising from the use of the Work, including but not limited to direct, indirect, incidental punitive and consequential damages.

The Authors and the Publisher specifically disclaim any implied warranties of merchantability or fitness for any particular purpose and shall in no event be liable for any loss or profit or other commercial damage, including but not limited to special, incidental, consequential, or other damages incurred as a result of specific decisions made by the Reader and or User.

Publisher does not take responsibility for any Author- or third-party websites or their contents.

It is assumed that a Reader and or User reads books front to back and therefore start at the front flowing through the Disclaimer. This means that the Reader and or the User of the Work has entered into a "contract" with the Publisher that includes that the Reader and or User read and or used the contents and its information in the Work with full knowledge of and agreement with the Disclaimers.

Acting affirmatively or continuing to read and or use the Work is deemed by the Publisher that the Reader and or User accepts the terms and conditions of the Work and or its Disclaimers. If the Reader and or User of the Work refuse to accede to the terms of any of the Disclaimers contained herein, then it is agreed by the Reader and or User that the Reader and or User shall immediately return the Work. If the Reader and or User do not so act, the Publisher may argue that a "contract" was formed with the Reader and or User making the Reader and or User bound by the terms of the Disclaimers.

If the Disclaimers are defective in some way, or that the Disclaimers are defectively placed, the use of all Disclaimers will nevertheless in all instances still act as a claim to a defense.

If a claim, action, or proceeding is brought against the Publisher, its licensees, or any seller of the Work, based on facts which, if true, would violate any of the warranties or representations in this Agreement, Publisher may defend the same through counsel it chooses and may settle the same in its sole discretion.

AUTHOR'S DISCLAIMER

The Authors assert the following in regards to the book ("the Work") and the cover ("the Cover"):

Caution is advised when reading or using the Work. The Authors are not responsible for any damages sustained by the Reader ("the Reader") or User ("the User") of the Work, when reading or using the Work. The Authors shall not be responsible for any aspect that may result in claims of defamation and invasion of privacy. In all instances, and as far as is reasonably possible, the Authors have relied on third party representations and expertise.

It is assumed that a Reader and or User reads books front to back and therefore start at the front owing through the Disclaimer. This means that the Reader and or the User of the Work has entered into a "contract" with the Author that includes that the Reader and or User read and or used the contents and its information in the Work with full knowledge of and agreement with the Disclaimers.

Acting affirmatively or continuing to read and or use the Work is deemed by the Author that the Reader and or User accepts the terms and conditions of the Work and or its Disclaimers. If the Reader and or User of the Work refuse to accede to the terms of any of the Disclaimers contained herein, then it is agreed by the Reader and or User that the Reader and or User shall immediately return the Work. If the Reader and or User do not so act, the Author may argue that a "contract" was formed with the Reader and or User making the Reader and or User bound by the terms of the Disclaimers.

If the Disclaimers are defective in some way, or that the Disclaimers are defectively placed, the use of all Disclaimers will nevertheless in all instances still act as a claim to a defense.

If a claim, action, or proceeding is brought against the Authors, its licensees, or any seller of the Work, based on facts which, if true, would violate any of the warranties or representations in this Agreement, the Authors may defend the same through counsel it chooses and may settle the same in their sole discretion.

Contents

PREFACE

On December 1969, Robert Seamans of the United States Air Force, after nearly 22 years, following the reccomendation of the Air Force sponsored UFO study committee at the University of Colorado. The report of the University commitee was issued in and dessension within the commitee itself. The chairman concluded that further scientific work on the problem held little promise of cogent scientific value and reccommended early in 1969 that the air force discontinue futher concern with the problem, although it was thought the UFO stories to die out, it increased even more daily...

From the closing of Project Sighn came the opening of another UFO phenomen project known as Project Gruge into a later name decided as project grudge... From here the ufo sightings went down, two years later the project was given up again, encforth came the insparation of rapid ufo sightings being made, this time project blue book came into existence, this time by Scientists from all over the world came to undertake the most difficult task of their lives...to prove if UFOs actually existed.

Three years later of hard work and brain shattering discoveries they came back from werever they had been, from their coming back not aword was spoken about the UFO crisis, in fact the files on which their facts had been set on, were destroyed, but a few American Agents managed to find out about what had been found before the files had been destroyed...

NOTES

NOTES

NOTES

NOTES

TOP SECRET

2-5317.

USAFE 14

TT 1524 TOP SECRET

From OI OB

4 Nov 1948

For some time we have been concerned by the recurring reports on flying saucers. They periodically continue to cop up; during the last week, one was observed hovering over Neubiberg Air Base for about thirty minutes. They have been reported by so many sources and from such a variety of places that we are convinced that they cannot be disregarded and must be explained on some basis which is perhaps slightly beyond the scope of our present intelligence thinking.

When officers of this Directorate recently visited the Swedish Air Intelligence Service. This question was put to the Swedes. Their answer was that some reliable and fully technically qualified people have reached the conclusion that "these phenomena are obviously the result of a high technical skill which cannot be credited to any presently known culture on earth." They are therefore assuming that these objects originate from some previously unknown or unidentified technology, possibly outside the earth.

One of these objects was observed by a Swedish technical expert near his home on the edge of a lake. The object crashed or landed in the lake and he carefully noted its azimuth from his point of observation. Swedish intelligence was sufficiently confident in his observation that a naval salvage team was sent to the lake. Operations were underway during the visit of USAFE officers. Divers had discovered a previosuly uncharted crater on the floor of the lake. No further information is available, but we have been promised knowledge of the results. In their opinion, the observation was reliable, and they believe that the depression on the floor of the lake, which did not appear on current Hydrographic charts, was in fact caused by a flying saucer.

Although accepting this theory of the origin of these objects poses a whole new group of questions and puts much of our thinking in a changed light, we are inclined not to discredit entirely this somewhat spectacular theory, meantime keeping an open mind on the subject. What are your reactions?

T O P S E C R E T

(END OF USAFE ITEM 14)

NOTES

NOTES

NOTES

NOTES

NOTES

NOTES

UFO sightings made only in California & Washington from 1947 to 1969:

YEAR:	NO:	YEAR:	NO:
""47	79	""59	364
""48	143	""60	514
""49	186	""61	488
""50	169	""62	474
""51	121	""63	399
""52	1,501	""64	526
""53	425	""65	887
""54	429	""66	1,060
""55	404	""67	937
""56	778	""68	392
""57	1,178	""69	146*
""58	590	(""*" ")146* Results uncomplete	

TAKEN FROM ACTUALL Project Blue book File

NOTES

NOTES

NOTES

NOTES

NOTES

NOTES

NOTES

NOTES

Page 9 UNCL...

I have received lots of requests from people who told me to make a lot of wild guesses. I have based what I have written here in this article on positive facts and as far as guessing what it was I observed, it is just as much a mystery to me as it is to the rest of the world.

My pilot's license is 333487. I fly a Callair airplane; it is a three-place single engine land ship that is designed and manufactured at Afton, Wyoming as an extremely high performance, high altitude airplane that was made for mountain work. The national certificate of my plane is 33365.

Kenneth Arnold
Box 587
Boise, Idaho.

traveling this way

Top

They seemed longer than wide their thickness was about 1/20 of their width

Mirror Bright

They did not appear to me to whirl or spin but seemed in fixed position traveling as I have made drawing.

Kenneth Arnold.

17

NOTES

INTRODUCTION

The story you are about to read is s trictly fictious,all characters involved in thisnovel have been made out of the mind.This story has no connection what so ever with the countries involved,the purpose of this book is to develope the UFO mystery no longer. In fact the story your going to read will give you the basic background to the project undertaken by the USA government to prove the true identity behind the UFO crisis...

Join us now as we search for the mystery behind the UFO's

Originally designated project Sighn,the investigative efort became project Grudge shortly theraft er,but for the major portion of its existence was known as project Blue Book...

CHAPTER One

Keeping a signal from the world

During the second world war unexplained balls of light which occasionaly appeared to accompany planes on bombing missions appeared very often to pilots, here is a recent advent, very recent in fact with a civilian pilot Kenneth Arnold...

"IM descending on 184, over"Kenneth Arnolds smooth but priscly voice rang out over the microphone on the control tower in a small hut like place, with only a few men at the controls. "We read you, over"Said a thick moustache mexican who had just taken a sip from a cup of cofee lying on the table next to him.

On board the small plane, Kenneth Arnold adjusted the instruments and dials in front of him as he made contact with the tower once more. "I have full contact, reading you on channel 90 wavelength three, over"He said slowly has he read his radar, then he saw something flash across his screen, several objects were visible on it, then suddenely they dissapeared out of sight.

"What was that ? "Asked the main headman as he too saw the objects cross the small green screen. Kenneth Arnold had already been flying for half an hour over Mt Rainer in Washington. All the men came towards the moud moustached man.

"Come in Arnold, we have confirmation of a TWA L-ten eleven your six o clock position, fifteen miles and an Alleghency DC-4 your twelve o clock fifty miles. Stand by one. Let me take a look at your broadband"

On the commputer tables all the reflections of the radar scoops changed from narrow band to broadband normal radar, the objects with crescentlike appearances could be seen again. "There is definetly a non-beacon target overhead fifty miles in your vicinity, slightly above and descending towards you, Unidentified flying object approaching and flying at a low altitude, has the brightest anti-collision lights ive seen...and the colours, are absolutely striking appearences..."

Kenneth Arnolds voice in exitment suddenely rang in from the other side of the interphone. "I can see them, theyre several objects with colours which almost blind, its fantastic, ive never seen such a thing, its like torpedoes ,traveling around by themselves."

Then another man spoke at the intercome, "Confirm, your Alltitude, we have a no go signal here"His hard and cold voice broke out.

"I suddenely have negative and affirmative reading, over"

"You have alot of static up there over..."No answer

"Come in Arnold..."

No answer

But then a sort of static sound and then..."Im safe, ive landed..."

Everyonem in the green lit control room tower, sighed with relief, they had seen a UFO .

THIS was said to have been the starting of the UFO crisis in 1947...

Five years later after Project BLUE BooK...

"Hi there"Said a man with white hair coming over to the other with dark hair.

"Hi, there Stephen"Shouted the dark haired man called James Cook who was an highly qualified officer for the United States NAVY, Stephen Rankine had been an officer for the Air Force. "Long time, no see"Said James as he hugged his freind in the middle of the crowds in a restaurant. "Well, well who'd think of meeting you here, of all places" Responded Stephen.

"Join me, im just about to start grazing"James spoke.

"Stephen, joins no one, when his on duty"Said Stephen.

"You mean your on duty ?"

"Yep, Ill have to join you some other time, perhaps will meet again"Stephen said and ran out again.

Two weeks later, one evening at James cooks apartment a telephone buzz came over. James answered it. "Yep"

A hurried and tired voice came over the air, suddenely James recognised it has Stephens voice, he seemed very rushed "James, is that you ?"

"Yes, whats wrong ?"

"Youve got to help me, Im in trouble, big trouble, remmember that project which was based on those UFO mysteries, called Project Blue Book, well its all a fake, I know all about it, I know who is be..." The note of thrillment ended there by a noise, a loud noise, like a gun shot.

"Stephen ?" Asked James staring at the phone in amazement.

"Stephen ?" Shouted James this time. "Stephen ?" He repeated.

He put the phone down slowly, and at the same time shrugged.

Only a few seconds later had he clicked, his freind had been shot.

A worried James Cook went to work the next morning, thinking of the nights avent. At his parking place two men in grey coats came to meet him. "Were CIA-Agents, come with us" Said a squashed nosed man.

"Sure, sure" James answered. He went along with the men in the coats.

At the Police (CIA) station James had to answer a few questions, concerning his freind. "Your freind was found dead last night, eight shots in his back, hit by a 45'er, do you or are you envolved in this mess ?" Asked the chief of the CIA, he was a long, dark haired man with huge sideburns, he moved in mechanical like movements.

"No, I am not involved at all, I got a telephone call last night frommy freind who..." James was interupted suddenely. "What business did this conversation concern, or was it not important, and...if it was'nt very important why was he shot eight times in his back" Asked the chief inspector.

"He talked to me about something, It was so rapid I didnt have time to state my confirmative data"

"Quit joking and give me all you heard"

James thought positive now, should he tell them everything he heard about, but then he had athought, they could easily trace the phone call, he thought again.

"All I heard was something about an, well, I dont know, Im sorry..." James found it easy to pass in that story as an excuse, a bit of acting as he had done at Drama school saved him, he knew for himself he would have to find the murderer and what Stephen Had found, it was just like his school days, only this time it was real. How would he Tackle the mystery the mystery of Project Blue Book.

James Cook was free to go an hour later but he now tried to go to the air force, he could possibly find something there.

James had to show his ID card at the USAF gate to the gaurd standing in neatly pressed Uniform.

His small car parked outside the main door into the USAF office's.

At the reseptionist, he asked for Major Robert Seamans JR of the United States Air Force. He was told to report to section one, priority one area 3 department xp. At the location given to him at the entry he found Major Robert Seamons Jr who had led the UFO project called Project Grudge and Part of Project Sighn, also he led the BLUE book which had taken place six years ago.

James came towards The major who sat on a skin chair with alot of paperwork in front of him, outside the noise of buzzing engines of small planes could be heard.

The major looked up, his green eyes staring at him tensely.

"Yes ?" Asked Robert Seamans Jr.

James looked behind him and the door closed.

"I want to Talk to you major, about Project Blue Book."

The major gave an astonished Expression. "I have no priority on those top secret files, in fact I had word a few days ago the files were destroyed"

"Now, sir, dont give me that, I learned that you had been in charge of the whole project."

"What the hell do you wont ? "Asked the major standing.

"What I wont to ask you is, why has Project Blue book been so damn secret."

"Why should I tell you, your no relation of mine, or a close freind." The major said and was about to switch the button for an officer to throw him out. "Dont do that, Major, I think you'd better talk to me about that project of yours"

"Why ? "Shouted the major.

"Because, major Seamans, it cost the life of my freind, and I wont to find out why"

"Your freind ? "Asked the major pulling out a chair for James. "I think we'd better talk about this whole matter.

About ten minutes later after James had explained who he was and his story the major did'nt now what to do, he ran his fingers through his hair in desbelief. "I dont know, I realy dont know what to do" He said worridely.

"Well, Major. Tell me all about Project Blue Book and ILL leave you alone" James interupted. "Well, its strictly top Secret, and not for only that but it was actually even kept from the world" The major said switching on the kettle and filling it with fresh water.

"You mean it was that secret, you mean they found something so secret, they didnt reveal it" James asked. "But Stephen must have found out what the secret was, why else would they shot him, he said that the project was all a fake, now I dont understand, you think theres probably some connection, some fraud, probably the biggest fraud in history? "Asked James trying out his imagination.

The major came over to James with two cups of coffee, he handed him one and took a sip from the other, he gave a plate of old, rock hard biscuits to James, James took one and looked at the major still in his thoughts. "Mr Cook, I have decided to help you, not with information concerning Project BLUE BOOK, but trying to persuade the university letting me go over a few of the files, no promises"

When James came out of the Majors office, two men in grey coats came to him again, they held out their ID cards, it read LAPD, he followed the men to the CIA station. At the station the same sargent came to him. "What is it this time ? "Asked James sarcastically.

"We wont you to identify your freinds body, and answer a few questions later on" The sargent said leading James into a white room with body cabinets, a man pulled out a stretcher like thing with a body under a white cloth covered from head to toe, a little tag on his big toe. The man pulled back the white cloth slightly to reveal a mans body, badly beated and bullet holes right through his body. James stared in amazement. "Thats not Stephen" Said James, now he was realy stuck, were would he turn to, where was Stephen, What was his next move.

"You mean, that is not your freind, Stephen Rankine ? "Asked the Sargent, placing the cloth back on the body, the man pulled the strecher back in the compartment again.

"No it is not my freind, but then who is he? "James said puzzled.

He then was led into the Sargents office.

After he had answered all the questions which the sargent had asked, except for those questions which delt with Project Blue Book, he consulted the major about Stephen and the other body they had found. What puzzled James now was, the voice that he had heard that night of the murder, the voice he heard was Stephens definetly, no one could immitate his voice so perfectly.

That Afternoon he left on a plane for Colorado, the University of Colorado.

When the plane touched down, he had a quick lunch and then he rented an hotel.

The next day he rented a car and headed for the University where the Project Blue Book files would be allocated and found, with a little hard work he thought he would be able to see the files, this was easier said than done.

NOTES

NOTES

NOTES

NOTES

NOTES

NOTES

NOTES

NOTES

NOTES

NOTES

NOTES

NOTES

NOTES

CHAPTER Two

N.A.S.A.s LINK to BLUE BOOK

At the University of Colorado, James Cook was to find bad news about the project files. When he entered the huge University he headed directly to the main conference chambers were he would find the men behind the UFO crisis and the*Condon Reports.
He walked through the vast complex of the huge University until he reached chamber 19 were he could find what he was looking for, the men that ensured every up to date recording Data of the Condon Reports after the project blue book had been made...
At an entry way he asked for Dr. Johnson one of the men involved in Blue book, he was given a location. At chamber 99824 room 746 he entered and there he found a black bearded man with square spectacles. From Dr. Johnson he was shown around and learned that only the non-important information had been kept, the rest had been destroyed two days ago, he also told him that a man managed to steel some files before they were totally destroyed and if the files were shown around, the third world war would start.
James asked him two questions.
"Whats this about the third world war?"
"Nothing realy, forget everything you heard"
"Did you recognise the man that stole the files ?"
"I didnt see his appearence but from men that saw him, they say he had white hair and probably brown eyes, six foot five and wore rushian clothes."
"Rushian clothes?"
"I dont know"
"Tell me something, how secret was this Project, project Blue Book, I mean."
"Well Id say it was pretty secret, after all the files were kept at NASA base 51 somewhere near the caribean islands in Radioactive containers, and those containers were kept in superflamable chambers 300 leagues under water."
"That secret?"
"Yep, you can say that"
"Thanks for your co-operation, Dr Johnson, before I go, do you mind letting me keep the rest of the files that are left, those non-important I mean."
"Sure"

After looking over the files he handed them back, he had found nothing except a few dates and some data on UFO's. He then drove to the nearest Nasa station, there he confronted some men involved in Project Grudge and a few of Sighn. After having a serious discussion with UFO experts and radar men about UFO sightings they had made, he was still in square one.
He had learned nothing this time.

That night he booked a flight to Russia after having learned that Project Blue book files had been kept their for good purposes.
The next morning he left and 15 hours later he was in Moscow, from there he booked an hotel and got a room at an expensive hotel/restaurant. He also made contact with the navy to inform them he would, be back soon...he hoped.
Just has James was about to get into bed his phone rang, he picked it up
"Yes?"
"We have your freind Stephen, if you wont to see him alive meet me at Kanoererest corner in an abandonded warehouse"The phone went dead.
"Hullo?"
No answer.
He got out of his warm feathered bed.

At the corner he was given to meet the other man he parked his car and walked out slowly into the dark and into the warehouse in the distance,when he came in the warehouse he looked around,there was no sighns of life,then something moved,it was a small mouse he smiled and then a light of a flashlight blinded his eyes,suddenely something hit him, he went unconscoious....

....when he awoke he was on a chair looking straight at Stephen,his eyes weary,his hands tied behind his back,his wrists sour and his body was shaky,he looked around,only Stephen,on a desk a pile of papers,he then saw he was in a cave,outside ice clung to the windows and snow carpeted the ground a few feet. It was dark,on a wall was a watch,it read 11o clock.

He whispered:

"Stephen,Stephen,can you here me"

Stephen was still out,his sleeve was pulled up and on the floor a siringe with clear liquid. was visible,a few books filled the small cabin.

James tried untying the ropes behind his back,he couldnt,the ropes were to tight,that they even cut through his skin.

A lamp in the middle of the desk lit the room and a few cards were lying next to it.

Suddenely the cabin door came open and the cold from the outside came in,James closed his eyes slightly.A man in Skies and orange ski-suit with a brownish beard came in,James recognised him instantely,the man with the square spectacalsknown to James has Dr.Johnson came in with snow all over his beard.

"I know your awake,Mr.Cook"Said Johnson who came to him.

James opened his eyes.

"Lets talk,shall we?"Johnson spoke.

"Why you?"James asked wearily "Why in blazes,you?"

"I have been a russian spy in America for four years and no one has suspected me,they trained us well"

"They?"Yes the SSPQ"

Stephen suddenely flicked his eyes open,Johnson saw it and said:

"Good,two is better than one to answer all questions."

After having suffered and answered a few questions,they were untied and they were taken at gun point into the night,they skied until they got to a huge ridge,ther they stopped and Johnson pressed a button on his belt,the ground heeved upwards and a trap door opened upwards. Stephen looked at James,they had'nt talked yet but they soon would.

They went underground in silence,the walls became modern and then echoes of their feet sounded through the corridors,a secret wall opened in front of them upwards and before their eyes they saw the most unbelievable scene of their lives. In front of them was the biggest hall they had ever seen with eight by eight foot round flat plates on the roofs this were the UFOs that had fooled mankind for countless years,men underneath in Macdonald suits filled every spacing."this round discs,have fooled everyone for centuries,only 22% of the UFOs are genuine arcticles the rest are satalites produced by us theSSPQ."

James looked at Stephen"We mustnt let them carry on with this,we must stop them,even if we die,for the sake of the world,they wont let us live anyway"

"Stop whispering you two"Johnson said has he came closer to them.

"You see those small fire lamps on the desks?"James asked."When I say go knock them down as quick as you can and lets try and get out of here"

The activity in the hall went down as James shouted "NOW"

They hit the desks and fire blazed everywhere,they managed to get out the way they came in. Huge gigantic flames licked every scrap of machinery in the huge hall,Suddenely the whole thing burst into a million vioid bulb of explosive hell...

Stephen didnt survive but James came out with a few scratches and burns.

He went walking through the snow and grizzly bears and hungry foxes waited for him,he accomplished what he had to do for the sake of the world,even if he would not survive, fraud UFOs wouldnt also,perhaps one day man would make contact with genuine UFOs...

PROLOGUE

The story you have read is just a story and nothing else,but let it not be confused with real events of the world history,if the story you have read ever comes true,it is purely a coinsidence,but were still back to square one,do UFOs realy exist,no one knows only(perhaps) the people that were behind Project Blue book...
Is'nt it time we were told the truth and nothing but the truth even if it is tinged with fear...

This story has been written with thanks to the United States government on contribution with the Project BLUE BOOK files.

Ther is plenty more to this story still to come...

THE END

NOTES

NOTES

NOTES

NOTES

NOTES

NOTES

NOTES

NOTES

NOTES

NOTES

NOTES

NOTES

NOTES

NOTES

NOTES

NOTES

NOTES

NOTES

NOTES

NOTES

www.ingramcontent.com/pod-product-compliance
Ingram Content Group UK Ltd.
Pitfield, Milton Keynes, MK11 3LW, UK
UKHW050613260726
13967UKWH00008B/2842

9 781105 734724